D0559341

Martin Bridge
Onwards and Upwards!

Illustrated by
Joseph Kelly

Written by
Jessica Scott
Kerrin

Kids Can Press

To Peter and Elliott, along with special thanks to all the people who have reviewed the Martin Bridge books, including Robin Smith of *The Horn Book Magazine*. Much appreciation! — J.S.K.

For Puddy, = ^..^ = — J.K.

Text © 2009 Jessica Scott Kerrin
Illustrations © 2009 Joseph Kelly

All rights reserved. No part of this publication may be reproduced, stored in a retrieval system or transmitted, in any form or by any means, without the prior written permission of Kids Can Press Ltd. or, in case of photocopying or other reprographic copying, a license from The Canadian Copyright Licensing Agency (Access Copyright). For an Access Copyright license, visit www.accesscopyright.ca or call toll free to 1-800-893-5777.

This is a work of fiction and any resemblance of characters to persons living or dead is purely coincidental.

Kids Can Press acknowledges the financial support of the Government of Ontario, through the Ontario Media Development Corporation's Ontario Book Initiative; the Ontario Arts Council; the Canada Council for the Arts; and the Government of Canada, through the BPIDP, for our publishing activity.

Neither the Publisher nor the Author shall be liable for any damage that may be caused or sustained as a result of conducting the activity in this book without specifically following instructions, or ignoring the cautions contained in the book.

Published in Canada by
Kids Can Press Ltd.
29 Birch Avenue
Toronto, ON M4V 1E2

Published in the U.S. by
Kids Can Press Ltd.
2250 Military Road
Tonawanda, NY 14150

www.kidscanpress.com

Edited by Debbie Rogosin
Designed by Julia Naimska
Printed and bound in Canada

Interior art was drawn with graphite and digitally shaded. Cover art was painted with acrylic and pixels.

The text is set in GarthGraphic.

The hardcover edition of this book is smyth sewn casebound.

The paperback edition of this book is limp sewn with a drawn-on cover.

CM 09 0 9 8 7 6 5 4 3 2 1
CM PA 09 0 9 8 7 6 5 4 3 2 1

**Library and Archives Canada
Cataloguing in Publication**

Kerrin, Jessica Scott
    Martin Bridge onwards and upwards! / written by Jessica Scott Kerrin ; illustrated by Joseph Kelly.

ISBN 978-1-55453-160-8 (bound).
ISBN 978-1-55453-161-5 (pbk.)

I. Kelly, Joseph II. Title.

PS8621.E77M366 2009   jC813'.6
C2008-903811-

Kids Can Press is a (©rUs™ Entertainment company

Contents

Meet ...

Polar Pete

Kyle

Head Badger Bob

Keyboard

Cripes, thought Martin as he and his mom
rounded the corner to the house of his
best friend, Stuart. Stuart's driveway was
blocked by Polar Pete's ice-cream truck, and
the truck had a *car* sticking out of its side.

Double cripes! The car belonged to
Stuart's mom, but she wasn't in it!

The car doors swung open, and two
boys scrambled out.

It was Stuart and Martin's other best
friend, Alex.

"Oh, my!" exclaimed Martin's mom as she pulled over to the curb. "Stay here," she ordered, and she jumped from the van.

Martin strained to watch from the window. No one appeared to be hurt. Polar Pete had turned off his musical bells and was checking the damage. And a lot of shouting and finger pointing was going on between Martin's two friends.

It wasn't long before Stuart's mom

dashed out of the house to the scene of the crash. The boys stopped fighting and sheepishly scuffed at the ground.

Martin's mom made her way back to the van.

"What happened?!" Martin demanded as she climbed in.

"It seems that Alex and Stuart were pretending they were flying in a rocket. One of them accidentally released the gear shift. The car rolled into the street and hit Polar Pete's truck as he was cruising by."

Triple cripes!

But Martin wasn't surprised. Alex was

always full of harebrained ideas, and he often dragged Martin and Stuart along for the ride.

"I guess they're in big trouble," said Martin.

"I would think so," replied his mom matter-of-factly.

She did a U-turn.

"So I won't be playing with them today," Martin concluded, making no effort to hide his disappointment about how his summer holiday was starting off.

Martin's mom was taking a couple of weeks of vacation to putter around the house, but Martin had set more ambitious goals. He and his friends planned to spend every day perfecting their skills at Zip Rideout's Space Race Game.

Zip Rideout, Space Cadet, was their favorite cartoon hero.

"Maybe you could call the boys later and see how they're doing," suggested Martin's mom. "Hey, isn't that a yard sale?"

Martin looked out his window and spotted the usual trademarks: a lawn covered with tables that displayed all kinds of potential treasure, along with barely used exercise equipment, outdated computers and antique baby cribs.

"I *love* a good yard sale!" sang Martin's mom as she pulled over.

They climbed out of the van and made their way to the nearest items.

It only took a few minutes of sifting through the clutter before Martin's mom came across an electronic keyboard.

"Oh, Martin! I've always wanted to learn to play."

She spotted the seller and called out boldly, "How much for the keyboard?"

Martin did not stick around for the answer. He quickly disappeared into the

milling crowd. Listening to his mom negotiate was excruciating. She was ruthless and could bargain anyone down to almost nothing.

Take the tape player she had picked up a few weeks ago. As Martin recalled, *that* conversation had been pure agony.

"How much for the tape player?"

"Ten dollars."

"Ten dollars!" she had haggled. "But it's so old! I'll give you ... fifty cents."

"*Fifty cents?* No way. How about eight dollars?"

"Eight? How about seventy-five cents?"

"*Seventy-five* cents? No can do ..."

And on and on.

"I paid a dollar-fifty for this tape player," she had bragged to Martin's dad when they got home. "Now we can play those old tapes we have boxed in the basement."

Martin's ears burned as he recalled the purchase. Come to think of it, she still hadn't hauled out those tapes.

Martin was leafing through a stack of *Zip Rideout: Space Cadet* comic books at a far table when she found him, the keyboard tucked under her arm.

"I'm practically stealing this," she whispered with excitement, her face flushed with the thrill of a good deal. "Do you want me to get those comics for you?"

she added generously.

"No!" said Martin, dropping the comics in haste. "I'm pretty sure I have these ones," he added as an excuse. "Let's go."

On the way home, Martin's mom made a detour and stopped by a music store to pick up some beginners' books.

"I can't wait to get started," she told Martin eagerly.

Martin thought that music in the house would be nice, but he was still distracted by the accident. He wondered how much trouble his friends were in.

As soon as he got in the door, Martin called Stuart.

"Hi, Stuart," said Martin. "How's it going?"

"Couldn't be worse," said Stuart miserably.

"I saw what happened with the ice-cream truck," admitted Martin. "At least no one was hurt."

"True. And Polar Pete's truck just needs some touch-up paint, so he'll be making rounds in no time. But there's a big dent in Mom's fender, Alex was sent home and *I'm* grounded," lamented Stuart. "I've got to think of a way to make it up to my mom."

"Maybe you could pay for the damage," suggested Martin.

"I don't have that much money!" Stuart protested.

"Maybe you could figure out how to earn some," said Martin.

Thick silence.

Finally, Stuart spoke. "You might be on to something. I'll talk to you later."

Martin called Alex next. His heart sank when he learned that Alex had also been grounded. With both friends out of commission, Martin felt like he was being punished, too!

Plink, plink. Plonk, plonk. Plink, plonk, plunk.

Martin's mom had begun to peck away

at the keyboard, which was front row center in the living room. It didn't sound as pleasant as Martin had expected. He went to check it out.

"I'm starting with 'Twinkle, Twinkle, Little Star,'" she announced proudly. "How does it sound?"

Martin's mom had no sense of rhythm, and the notes were all wrong.

"Sounds like this keyboard will be in our next yard sale, along with the tape player," Martin replied.

He could have been kinder, but having friends who were grounded soured his mood.

"Very funny," said his mom, undaunted. "You wait and see. I'll be playing like a pro in no time."

To Martin, it sounded as if she wasn't going to improve any time soon. And he felt a smidgen of sympathy for Mrs. Baddeck, his school's music teacher, who listened to beginner musicians all day long.

No wonder she rubbed her temples a lot.

"I'm going up to my room," declared Martin. His mom's enthusiasm for the keyboard was not infectious.

Martin thought he might glue the fins on his newest rocket. But the bothersome *plinking* and *plonking* drifted upstairs,

breaking his concentration.

He shut his door. It didn't help. He could still hear his mom struggling with "Twinkle, Twinkle" over and over and over.

It would be easier to listen to Alex and Stuart bickering over Zip Rideout's Space Race Game! Martin sprawled on his bed with a pillow over his head. And he hummed Zip's television theme song to further block her notes from entering his cocoon.

"I picked up a keyboard at a yard sale today," Martin's mom boasted to his dad at dinner. "I've been practicing all afternoon."

"Yes. *All* afternoon," repeated Martin, rolling his eyes.

"Well, then!" said Martin's dad jovially. "Can you play something for us? A little music to accompany dinner?"

Martin's mom leaped up from the table and bounded into the living room.

A mangled "Twinkle, Twinkle" wafted back to assault their ears.

Martin's dad listened intently, but looked confused.

"It's supposed to be 'Twinkle, Twinkle, Little Star,'" Martin whispered. He hoped that if his dad guessed it quickly, his mom would stop wrestling with the notes and they could eat in peace.

"'Twinkle, Twinkle'?" Martin's dad called out, giving Martin the thumbs-up.

Martin's mom returned to the kitchen.

"No," she answered. "I was working on 'Twinkle, Twinkle' earlier, but it was too hard. Now I'm learning 'Baa, Baa, Black Sheep.'"

There was an awkward pause, then Martin burst out laughing.

"What?" she asked.

"Well," said Martin's dad gently, stepping in while Martin recovered. "I think Martin's trying to tell you that 'Twinkle, Twinkle' and 'Baa, Baa, Black Sheep' are the same tune, just different words."

"I know that," said Martin's mom, spearing her peas in a way that told them she did not.

Martin's dad reached over and patted her hand.

"Look, you two," she said, "I may not be the best musician in the world, but I can certainly learn to play a few simple songs. Now, if you'll *excuse* me" — she picked up her dishes and rinsed them at the sink — "I have some practicing to do."

She disappeared into the living room.

Plink, plink, plonk went the notes.

"Maybe she should try a different instrument," said Martin, covering his ears.

"Actually, this isn't her first attempt," admitted Martin's dad. "Before you came along, there was the guitar, the trumpet and ... oh, yes, the violin."

"Cripes," said Martin.

"I can hear you in there!" Martin's mom called out.

But she kept on pecking away.

And when Martin got up for breakfast the next morning, she had already been practicing for an hour. He poured himself a bowl of Zip Rideout Space Flakes, but added less milk than usual. The extra crunching sound blocked out the killer background noise while he ate.

Martin called Alex right after breakfast.

"I thought of a way for Stuart and I to raise money to pay for his mom's fender," Alex announced proudly.

"How?" asked Martin.

His mom was still banging away, so Martin had to plug one ear with his finger to hear Alex.

"Remember the time when Curtis borrowed all the neighbors' water sprinklers?"

Curtis was Alex's little brother.

"Sure," said Martin. "He arranged them in your backyard to cheer you up when you had the chicken pox."

The waterworks had been spectacular.

But Martin was suspicious. Alex's enthusiasm had all the makings of yet another crazy scheme.

"Well, I was thinking that Stuart and I could do the same thing for birthday parties and stuff. Like those flocks of pink flamingos you see on lawns. Only, instead of birds, we'd set up sprinklers. People could hire us to do it as a surprise."

Martin did not think neighbors would *pay* to have surprise sprinklers set up in their front yards. He was about to tell Alex that his idea was all wet, when Alex abruptly changed the subject.

"What's that awful racket?" he demanded.

"My mom. She's learning how to play the keyboard," mumbled Martin.

"Holy cow!" exclaimed Alex. "Will she get any better?"

"I doubt it," Martin replied. "She's been practicing the same song forever. I think she's getting worse."

"Well, I can barely hear you. I'm going to call Stuart and tell him about my sprinkler idea."

Alex hung up, and Martin unplugged his ear. The barrage of notes filling the kitchen sounded just as bad to Martin as Alex's business scheme.

"Maybe you should take a break!" suggested Martin as he stomped by the living room.

"No breaks for me," replied his mom cheerily. "If I don't keep at it, I'll never get better."

Martin thought that only the *last* part of her statement was correct.

"Well, *I* sure need a break," he declared, and he escaped to his tree fort with some comics.

Martin's mom continued to plod away at the keyboard all day, so Martin had to endure the torture every time he went inside.

"Hey, Mom! Where'd you put my earplugs?" Martin shouted down from his room that evening after suffering through forty-five minutes of "Chopsticks."

Martin owned a pair of earplugs that he wore whenever he watched fireworks.

"In the bathroom cupboard, top drawer," she called back. "Am I still that bad?"

"Yes!" shouted Martin bluntly.

He knew he was being cruel, but his nerves were absolutely *shot*. She rarely got more than three or four notes right in a row!

"Well," she replied without any apology, "I guess I need to increase my practice time.

'Onwards and upwards,' as Zip would say."

Martin made no attempt to cover up his groan.

The next day, from the sanctuary of his tree fort, Martin heard the familiar jingle of ice-cream bells. Polar Pete had returned to making his daily rounds. Martin was only too pleased to rush inside and interrupt his mom's playing to ask for some change. He was dying to try Zip Rideout's new line of ice-cream flavors.

"What's that sound?" asked Polar Pete after Martin placed his order for Zip's Rocky Rocket Ripple.

"My mom's learning to play the keyboard,"

said Martin glumly. "She picked one up at a yard sale."

"Good for her!" exclaimed Polar Pete, handing the ice-cream cone to Martin. "Music brings such happiness."

"Not always," said Martin between licks. "Mom's music sounds best from my tree fort, where I can barely hear it."

"In time she'll get better," Polar Pete assured him. "Tell her from me to keep up the hard work."

Martin had no intention of conveying Polar Pete's message to his mom. But it *did* give Martin an idea. After some searching, he hauled the tape player, a fresh set of batteries and the box of old tapes up to his tree fort.

The first couple of recordings featured screechy guitars, but then Martin came across a funny song about being a walrus. He drew a picture of one while he played the song  over and over. When he was done, he climbed down and called Stuart.

"I'm going to join Alex in his sprinkler party business," Stuart informed Martin.

Martin was about to tell Stuart that no one would be crazy enough to trust Alex with a lot of water, but Stuart cut in.

"What's that horrible noise?"

"My mom. She's learning to play the keyboard," Martin grumbled.

"Ka-boom!" exclaimed Stuart. He always said that when something was about to go wrong.

Martin had the exact same thought about the sprinkler party partnership, but his mom's playing forced Stuart to hang up before Martin could tell *him* "Ka-boom!"

Martin returned to his tree fort to listen to more tapes. He came across another song he liked — about an octopus's garden. He drew that, too. Then he came down for his favorite

television show, *Zip Rideout: Space Cadet.*
He turned up the volume really loud,
forcing his mom to take a break.

"Maybe someday I could learn to play
Zip's 'Onwards and Upwards' theme song,"
suggested Martin's mom enthusiastically.

Martin took that as a threat. He quickly
switched to another channel in the hope
that she would learn to ruin the song of
some other show.

Over the next few
days, Martin worked his
way through the box of
tapes. And, every once
in a while, he came
across a terrific song,
like the one about a
yellow submarine.

When that happened, he'd get out his art supplies and set to work. The walls of his tree fort were nearly covered with underwater scenes.

Then, one morning, Martin climbed down from another tape session and went into the kitchen for a snack. As he stood staring at the contents of the fridge, he noticed that something was different.

Martin held his breath and listened hard.
Silence.

The only sound he could make out was his own nervous heartbeat.

Martin crept to the hallway, spylike, and peeked into the living room.

The keyboard stood alone. Had his mom finally figured out that she had no musical talent?

Fingers crossed, Martin returned to his tree fort.

Later in the afternoon, Martin made another daring mission to the kitchen. He wasn't even hungry. It was curiosity that drove him to it.

Once again, silence.

What was she up to?

Martin darted from room to room until he spied his mom sorting photos on her computer. He backed away and decided

not to mention the keyboard, in case it triggered a return of the practice sessions. But Martin did brave a conversation with Polar Pete.

"She's stopped playing," he confided over a scoop of Zip's Milky Way Mocha Swirl.

"What a shame," said Polar Pete.

But Martin was not yet convinced that his ordeal was over. Every time he entered the house that day and the next, he paused to listen, expecting the worst.

And every time, he was greeted by the glorious sound of nothing at all.

Then something strange happened.

Martin began to frown at the silence. Somehow, it had become eerie. He even started to wonder if he actually missed the *plink, plonk* of his mom's playing.

He replayed her tuneless tunes in his head.

No.

Her attempts at making music sounded just as bad in his memory as they had in real life.

Still, he couldn't shake the feeling that he was missing something.

Puzzled, Martin continued his spy missions. He watched his mom clipping articles from magazines, sorting the mail and tossing out dried-up bottles of nail

polish. But no matter what she was doing, she didn't look like she was having much fun.

"That's it!" Martin blurted as he lay in bed that night. It wasn't her music, it was her *excitement* about playing the keyboard that he missed. The house seemed emptier without it.

Martin bunched up his pillow at the thought of all those times he had stomped by the living room on the way to his tree fort. And then he remembered Polar Pete's words. Perhaps her happiness *was* worth putting up with a few badly played songs.

"Hi, Mom," said Martin when he searched the house the next morning and found her reading on the front porch. "How's the keyboard coming along?"

"The keyboard's not my thing," she declared, barely looking up.

"But you can still have fun with it. Polar Pete says you should keep up the hard work. Why don't you play something now?"

"I can't, Martin. I sold the keyboard.
Yesterday."

"What?!" exclaimed Martin. "You did?!"

He charged into the living room. A large
potted plant stood where the keyboard used
to be.

The air in the empty room was suffocating.

Martin slowly
returned to the porch
with something more
than thick silence
weighing heavily on
his shoulders.

"So, you're
quitting? Just like
that?" he asked in a
small voice.

"Well, it's not like
I didn't try. Besides, you must be getting
sick of 'Twinkle, Twinkle' by now."

Well, that was definitely true.

Still.

One uneasy question remained.
Martin wondered if he'd had anything to
do with her decision to sell the keyboard.

He studied his mom, who had returned to her book.

"Mom?" he asked hesitantly.

"Mmmmm?" she replied, turning a page.

More oppressive silence.

Martin struggled with his unspoken question, because he already knew the answer.

"Nothing," he mumbled.

The telephone rang.

"I'll get it," said Martin, and he went inside.

"Hello?"

"Hi, Martin," said Alex. "I've talked *everyone* into my sprinkler party business, and Stuart and I are starting this morning."

"Really?" said Martin, glad for the distraction.

"Yes," crowed Alex. "Harper's dad let us borrow the demo sprinklers from his hardware store. Kyle's dad printed business cards for us. And Clark's mom is giving us a table in front of her bakery to sell sprinkler party packages to people who buy her birthday cakes."

"How come you didn't ask *me* to help?" demanded Martin indignantly.

"You never offered!" said Alex.

He's right, thought Martin sadly. He had been too busy hating Alex's idea to even think about helping out.

Martin slumped against the wall. The heavy silence around him was replaced with stomach-churning guilt.

"Hey! I don't hear the keyboard," Alex remarked.

"It's gone," said Martin with regret.

But wait! Maybe there was a chance that he could still do something for his friends. He took a deep breath of that suffocating air.

"What about *decorating* your table?" Martin asked. "I could bring my new drawings of underwater stuff."

"That'd be great!" said Alex. "We're meeting at the bakery in an hour."

"Onwards and upwards!" Martin replied.

After he hung up, Martin stood, shoulders back. He knew that there would be few, if any, sprinkler party sales. But that didn't matter. Being supportive already felt way better than being right.

Bells rang faintly down the street. Martin rushed to the front porch and saw that his mom was already beside the ice-cream truck, chatting with Polar Pete.

Martin ran down to join them.

"I was just telling your mom about a drum set I saw up the street at a yard sale," explained Polar Pete as he handed a cone of Zip's Lunar Licorice Delight to Martin. "Your mom told me about the keyboard, but maybe drums are her thing."

"What do you think?" Martin's mom

asked eagerly, bending down to look Martin full in the face. "There's space in the living room where the keyboard used to be."

Her words were music to his ears.

Martin took only one quick lick of his ice cream, then said, "Let's go check them out."

Rope

Martin grudgingly shoved over as Laila Moffatt wedged herself between him and his two best friends, Alex and Stuart.

"I want to join the Junior Badgers," she announced.

"No, you don't," said Martin. He flipped open his starship lunchbox, determined not to give her idiotic comment a second thought.

"Yes, I do," she insisted, opening her lunchbox, too.

Laila's lunchbox featured an old-fashioned character named Rosie. She had a can-do look and was flexing her arm.

Martin glowered as Laila bit into her smelly tuna sandwich.

In class, Laila sat right in front of Martin. Her messy orange curls blocked his view of the blackboard. She was forever borrowing his pencil crayons. And whenever she got the right answer, which was a lot, she'd turn around and smile at him as if they shared a secret.

Martin's ears burned just thinking about it.

"Junior Badgers meet on Monday nights, right?" Laila asked, plowing ahead.

"So what if we do?" argued Stuart, coming to Martin's rescue. "You can't be serious about joining."

"I *am* serious," said Laila, chewing thoughtfully.

"Forget it, Laila," said Alex. "Junior Badgers are all about rocket launchings and surviving in the woods and building weapons. None of those are up your alley."

"Junior Badgers are also about earning badges," said Laila with deadly aim.

"Oh, so *that's* it!" exclaimed Martin. "You want to scoop all the badges! Don't you have enough awards and first-place ribbons?"

Laila generally cleaned up at the school's annual Awards Day. Martin imagined that her bedroom must be absolutely stuffed with prizes. The rest of the class had to scramble for leftovers like "most improved in spelling" or "teacher's helper" or "best debater."

Come to think of it, Laila had won "best debater" last year, too.

And it wasn't just winning awards that Laila was good at. She was a master organizer of team projects. She could beat Martin at his Zip Rideout Space Race

Game. And Martin knew that for someone her size, Laila was surprisingly strong.

He had made this last discovery after Laila had showed up a day late for his birthday, and Martin's mom had forced him to play with Laila in the backyard. Instead of taking the ladder, Laila had climbed all the way up to Martin's tree fort by rope to drop some water balloons.

Neither he nor his friends had ever climbed all the way up by rope.

It was just too hard.

And a little bit scary.

"You *can't* join the Junior Badgers, Laila," Stuart insisted, interrupting Martin's thoughts. "You don't even know the Junior Badger pledge."

Laila put down her sandwich, stood and recited the pledge flawlessly.

I promise with all my heart
To try new things with courage
And blaze ahead with honor
To learn something new every day
Especially from those around me.

Then she gave them the secret Junior
Badger salute.

All three boys gasped.

"How'd you know that?!" Martin
managed to ask, horrified by this breach in
troop security.

"Martin! I sit in front of you all day long.
How could I *not* know," she replied snootily.

Martin's best friends shot him death glares. He hung his head. Guilty as charged.

He bit into his cheese sandwich, which now tasted like sawdust. So did his favorite chocolate chip cookies.

At the next Junior Badger night, Alex elbowed Martin and pointed to the double doors of the lodge. Stuart looked, too.

There entered Laila in full Junior Badger uniform, an empty badge sash draped across her chest.

"She'll be adding badges to that sash in no time," Martin predicted grimly to Alex, who nodded in resentment.

Stuart clucked his tongue.

Laila scanned the hall, and when she spotted Martin, she gave him a cheerful wave.

Martin turned away, arms crossed. If Laila insisted on joining the Junior Badgers, that was one thing. But he sure wasn't going to make it easy for her to fit in.

No way.

"Attention, Junior Badgers!" boomed Head Badger Bob, the troop's leader. He waved a gigantic flag bearing the Junior Badger logo, which was the signal for everyone to form a circle for the opening burrow.

The Badgers quickly took their places and grew quiet. All eyes rested uneasily on Laila.

Martin could tell she was also on edge.

She had reached for her left foot and pulled it up behind her. Laila always did that when she was nervous.

Good! His earlier snub was working.

"I'd like everyone to give a warm Junior Badger welcome to our newest member," Head Badger Bob called out jovially.

Laila received a polite smattering of applause that quickly petered out.

"What's *she* doing here?" Kyle muttered to Martin.

Kyle was a year older than Martin, and he had only one more badge to earn before his sash was complete. A complete sash would mean that he'd receive high honors when he moved up to Trail Makers.

"Beats me," Martin replied, taking a step back.

Kyle's breath smelled like a dishcloth gone sour.

"Listen! This is no place for your brainiac friend," Kyle warned, wagging his finger in Martin's face.

"She's not my friend!" Martin protested.

"Tell her to stay away,"

insisted Kyle. "I'm *this* close" — he showed Martin the tiny gap between his thumb and pointer finger — "to filling my sash, and I don't need that brainiac taking up our Head Badger's marking time."

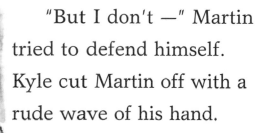

"But I don't —" Martin tried to defend himself. Kyle cut Martin off with a rude wave of his hand.

Fuming, Martin struggled to return his attention to Head Badger Bob. Laila stood across from him and grinned when she caught his eye.

He returned her friendliness with his fierce hands-on-hips stance.

It worked. She reached for her foot.

"As always, we'll start off by awarding the latest badges," announced Head Badger Bob.

Then he called out Martin's name. Martin eagerly stepped forward to receive his badge for bicycle safety.

Bicycle safety was one of the easier badges to complete. Many in the troop already had that one. But since Martin wasn't moving up to Trail Makers until next year, he was in no rush to get started on the harder badges.

After the awards, everyone took a seat on the floor.

"Tonight we have a special guest who will be teaching us about" — Head Badger Bob checked his clipboard — "oh, yes, *that's* the correct term. Scat!"

A man wearing a park ranger uniform
moved into the circle. Laila shot her hand
up into the air.

"What's scat?" she asked boldly.

"It's animal poop, Laila," explained
Head Badger Bob.

Laila frowned.

"Why would we want to learn about *that*?" she asked, wrinkling her nose.

"You can learn all kinds of things from studying scat," the park ranger cut in. "Like what wildlife eat, how healthy they are and where they've traveled."

Alex nudged Martin excitedly. Poop was right up Alex's alley.

And that was probably true for the rest of the troop, judging by the growing buzz.

The park ranger proceeded to show them all kinds of scat — owl, deer and even coyote.

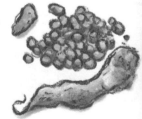

Laila pushed each new sample away with a
grimace, much to Martin's satisfaction.

The next morning at school, Martin
took his seat and tapped Laila's pointy
shoulder. She wheeled around and smiled.

"Hi, Martin," she said pleasantly.

"What did you think about the poop?"
Martin asked, knowing full well that she
had hated that activity.

"Not *poop*, Martin! Scat!" Laila corrected him. And then she added curtly, "I have no intention of quitting, if that's what you're thinking."

That was *exactly* what Martin was thinking. His ears burned.

"Besides," Laila continued, "I've already started working on several badges. Public Speaking. Journalism. And Good Citizenry." She counted them off on her fingers matter-of-factly.

Martin rolled his eyes. She was going straight for the hardest badges!

Typical.

On the next Junior Badger night, Laila showed up again, just as she had promised. And during the opening burrow, Head

Badger Bob made a big deal out of awarding
Laila the first badge on her ambitious list.

Laila beamed at Martin, still seeking his
approval. But Martin quickly turned away,
only to come face-to-face with Kyle.

Kyle did not look impressed.

After the opening burrow, everyone sat down.

"Tonight," boomed Head Badger Bob, "we'll be focusing on skills for outdoor survival. And as a special treat, we have a museum biologist on hand to teach us how to cook and eat ..."

There was a dramatic pause, and the Junior Badgers fidgeted in anticipation.

"... bugs!" finished Head Badger Bob gleefully.

"Holy cow!" exclaimed Alex, rubbing his hands together.

Eating bugs was right up Alex's alley.

Martin was thrilled, too. Laila had had a hard time handling last week's poop. He was positive that she would not be overjoyed about eating bugs.

Come to think of it, Martin wasn't so keen on eating them, either. But he'd do it if it would show Laila why she was not Junior Badger material.

All through the bug-cooking demonstration, Martin noticed that Laila was looking queasy and clutching her stomach.

"What's that know-it-all friend of yours still doing here?" snarled Kyle to Martin as the museum biologist began to serve the bugs.

Kyle's breath hadn't improved, and

now there was a hint of dirty-sock-at-the-bottom-of-the-hamper added to the sour dishcloth smell.

"How should I know?!" Martin replied, fighting the urge to plug his nose.

But Kyle persisted.

"Tell that keener to stay away from the badges," Kyle growled. "Like I said" — he held the space between his thumb and finger close to Martin's face — "I'm this close to completing my sash."

"I get it," said Martin flatly. "Have

some bugs," he added as the plate was passed around to their part of the circle.

"Delicious!" said Alex, who sat beside Martin, munching a handful. "Can I have seconds?" he earnestly asked their chef.

Martin gingerly picked the smallest bug he could find and quickly forced it down.

It tasted mostly of the spices that the museum biologist had added. Only the *thought* of eating bugs tasted really bad, Martin realized with surprise.

Triumphant, he looked across at Laila. A look of revulsion and horror swept over her face as she tried to swallow a bug. She jumped up and bolted to the washroom.

Martin smiled smugly.

The next morning in class, Martin tapped Laila on her pointy shoulder. This time, he thought he'd try a different approach to make her see that it was time to throw in the towel. Instead of grossing Laila out, he would pretend sympathy.

"I'm sorry about the bugs," Martin said in an apologetic tone. He shook his head

woefully to look even more convincing.

"I didn't like the bugs," Laila admitted. "But I'm not quitting, so you can forget it!"

Martin felt as if he had been hit in the stomach by a dodge ball.

"Besides," she continued. "I've added a few more badges to work on. Archaeology. Emergency Preparedness. And Soil and Water Conservation."

Martin's fake pity was replaced with genuine outrage.

"You're going for so many badges that Head Badger Bob won't have any time left to mark work from the rest of the troop!" Martin accused.

Laila shrugged off his outburst and turned to the front of the class.

Martin seethed.

Then he remembered Kyle's warning, delivered in that obnoxious breath of his.

Martin smoldered some more.

The next Junior Badger night, Laila received two more badges. If she kept going like that, she would catch up to Kyle in no time!

Martin hoped Kyle wouldn't notice, but his sinking heart told him there was no chance of that.

"Before we begin this evening's activities, I have an important announcement!" boomed Head Badger Bob as everyone sat down.

The Junior Badgers held their breath.

"The National Junior Badger Council has created a new badge to go with our pledge. It's called the Badge of Courage."

"The Badge of Courage," murmured the troop.

"Only this badge is a little different," explained Head Badger Bob. "With all the other badges, you prove to me that you are worthy of receiving them. With the Badge of Courage, members of your own troop must nominate you, and then I make the final decision, based on the nominations received."

"What does 'nominate' mean?" Alex whispered to Martin.

"It means to vote for someone," Martin whispered back.

"So you'll nominate me, right?" Alex replied without missing a beat. "Courage is right up my alley."

"Hang on," said Stuart, who had been

listening in. "I'm plenty courageous, too. I think Martin should nominate *me!*"

Martin said nothing. He hardly considered either of his two best friends courageous.

Take the time that Alex and Stuart had tried to get out of rescuing their class parakeet, Polly, from a junior high school. Or the time they made a big show of signing up for lead roles in the school play, only to back out at the last minute, leaving Martin to sing solo. And then there was the time they went to their superhero's movie premiere, *Zip Rideout and the Revenge of Crater Man,* but covered their eyes during the terrifying opening scene.

Kyle cut in. His breath was diabolical.

"You're all nominating *me,*" threatened

the older boy in barely a whisper.

"I'm" — he showed the impossibly
small gap between his thumb and finger —

"this close to completing my sash. I only need one more badge to get high honors, and I'm all out of the easy ones."

"There's still Archaeology," said Martin dryly. "Or Emergency Preparedness. Or Soil and Water Conservation."

"Are you nuts?!" Kyle demanded, glaring at Martin. "Those badges are *hard*! They'd take *forever*!"

Martin fanned away the ghastly breath with his hand. He wondered if Kyle ever brushed his teeth.

Head Badger Bob started to hand out the nomination forms.

"Each Badger can
only nominate one other Badger.
You'll see that you have to explain how
the Badger you nominate demonstrates
courage. Only one Badge of Courage will
be awarded per troop each year, so this
badge is very special."

Martin studied his form. There were an

awful lot of
blanks to fill out.
Then he scanned
the members of
the circle. He'd
have to nominate
someone. But
whom?

"Get these
nominations
back to me in
two weeks so that I'll have time to review
them before our move-up-to-Trail Makers
ceremony. That is," he continued jovially,
but looking directly at Laila, "if I'm not
swamped with other badges to mark."

Kyle leaned toward Martin again, his
breath a lethal weapon. "Hey! How come

that whiz-head friend of yours is still here?"
Martin snapped.

"I told you! For the hundredth time!
Laila is *not* my friend!" he shouted. "And for
the record, I don't want her here, either!"

Everyone sitting in the circle stopped
talking and stared at him.

Including Laila.

Her face went beet red.

Serves her right, thought Martin doggedly, fists clenched. The sooner she figures out that she doesn't belong here, the better. And if he had to be the one to come right out and say so, well that was fine. At least now, Kyle would get off his back.

The awkward silence was broken when Head Badger Bob cleared his throat.

"Perhaps it might be a good time to recite the Junior Badger pledge," he observed.

He always suggested that whenever someone in the troop went off track.

Together, everyone stood and dutifully recited the pledge. Martin, still unrepentant, shoved his fists in his pockets and only mouthed the words.

"Now I'd like to introduce tonight's special guest," announced Head Badger Bob as everyone sat down. "He's the president of the local reptile society, and he's brought some live specimens to show us."

The reptile expert pushed into the circle carrying several pillowcases with the ends knotted. The pillowcases squirmed when he put them down, much to the troop's delight.

Martin glanced at Laila. She had pulled her knees to her chest, making herself as small as possible.

The special guest carefully untied the knots one at a time. Out came snakes in all kinds of patterns and colors. And everybody held one except Laila, who adamantly refused when it was her turn.

"Watch this," said Kyle menacingly to Martin.

He sneaked up behind Laila and lightly
squiggled his fingers against her neck, as if
a snake had gotten loose.

Laila screamed and screamed as she
frantically tried to brush it away.

The troop exploded into laughter,
Martin included.

But it wasn't nearly as funny to Martin when, moments later, Kyle did the same thing to him.

"Get it off me!" Martin shouted, pawing at the back of his neck.

This brought about a second round of hysterical laughter.

"Very funny," muttered Martin when he realized he'd been duped. His ears burned with humiliation.

And for the first time, Martin felt a little sorry for Laila.

When the troop gathered for the next

Junior Badger evening, Kyle pounced.

"Hey, Martin!" he called, making sure that Head Badger Bob was out of earshot.

Head Badger Bob was at the far end of the lodge, going over plans with that night's special guest, a military historian.

"Guess you and Laila won't be getting the Badge of Courage any time soon," Kyle mocked.

Then he began to scream and go berserk the way Martin and Laila had

done during last week's fake snake prank.

Badgers doubled over with peals of laughter, while Martin filled with enough anger for both he *and* Laila.

Laila said nothing. She clasped her left foot, but by now she had stopped looking to Martin for acceptance.

If only Laila would quit, Martin thought with bitterness, this would all go away.

Yet even though the solution was simple, he

knew that Laila wouldn't quit. That she *couldn't* quit. She simply did not know how. She was going to keep coming week after week after week, snapping up badges left and right, while Kyle continued to make life miserable for her.

And for Martin.

There's no way out, thought Martin glumly.

And then he spotted the rope circuit.

The rope circuit was an awe-inspiring tangle

of lines and cables that towered at their end of the lodge. It was reserved for the Trail Makers, so members in Martin's troop hadn't trained on it yet.

That meant there was only one Junior Badger brave enough to make it to the top.

Martin took hold of the rope.

"Kyle's wrong!" he announced boldly. "Laila's got plenty of courage. Just watch her climb this rope."

Laila seemed confused by Martin's sudden show of support. She did not let go of her foot.

"No way she can do it," Kyle retorted loudly, just as Martin knew he would.

The doubters in the crowd began to chuckle.

"Oh, she can do it all right," Martin

boasted, still holding the rope out to her. "Onwards and upwards," he added.

It was something Zip Rideout said at the start of every mission.

Laila dropped her foot and beamed at Martin.

"Get out of my way, Kyle," she demanded, grabbing the rope.

By the time Kyle let out his first guffaw, Laila was halfway up. By the time he wiped the smirk off his face, Laila had reached the top and was on her way back down.

Alex elbowed Martin. "How'd you know she could do *that*?" he asked in wonder.

"Laila sits in front of me all day long. How could I *not* know?" replied Martin.

He gave her the Junior Badger salute when she touched the ground in lickety-split time.

Laila smartly returned the gesture.

That evening, the troop's special guest taught them how to build catapults. It was exciting to hurl objects, but the conversation

amongst Badgers kept
returning to Laila's
amazing rope feat.

"Will this fling water
balloons?" Laila asked
the military buff as he
came around to check
on everyone's work.

Smiling, Martin recalled the afternoon
that he and Laila had spent together
exploding water balloons from his tree fort.

A few weeks later, Laila was awarded
the Badge of Courage, much to Kyle's
disappointment. Almost all of the Junior
Badgers had nominated her because of her
impressive climb.

But that's not why Martin had filled out
Laila's name on *his* form. His nomination had

more to do with how she had kept coming back to Junior Badgers week after week.

Even when she had to look at scat.

Even when she had to eat bugs.

Even when she had been terrified by snakes.

And most difficult of all, even when she knew that no one had wanted her there.

"Courage is right up Laila's alley," Martin had written. And he had underlined his words.

Build a Marshmallow Catapult!

After Martin learned the basics about catapults at Junior Badgers, he built his own version, for acting out Zip Rideout's famous battle scenes. You can make one, too. Just take care with your aim!

You will need:

- 1 2-liter (2-quart) milk carton
- 3 pencils
- 1 plastic spoon
- assorted elastic bands
- 1 toothpick
- scissors (use with care for all cutting)
- ruler and felt marker
- mini marshmallows

1. Cut top off the milk carton, so that all four sides are 20 cm (8 in.) high.

2. *Back panel:* On one side, draw two horizontal lines, one at 3 cm (1 1/4 in.) and one at 6 cm (2 1/2 in.) from the bottom.

3. Cut two corner seams from top of carton down to line at the 3 cm (1 1/4 in.) mark. Then cut across line at the 6 cm (2 1/2 in.) mark. Discard panel. Fold resulting flap to the inside.

Back panel

4. *Front and side panels:* Draw a horizontal line 10 cm (4 in.) from the bottom of each of the other three sides. Cut corner seams down to that line. Fold resulting three flaps to the inside. The frame is now complete.

Front panel

Side panels

5. *Throwing arm:* Place one pencil behind the other, so that center of horizontal pencil crosses vertical pencil (throwing arm) near its eraser end. Crisscross an elastic band tightly around pencils to fasten them together. Loop a small elastic band to eraser end of throwing arm. The smaller the elastic band, the stronger the catapult!

Throwing arm

6. *Pivot:* Using pointy scissor end, drill a hole 4 cm (1 1/2 in.) from top and in middle of both side panels. Slide horizontal pencil into holes.

Pivot

7. *Brake:* Drill a hole 2 cm (3/4 in.) down and 2 cm (3/4 in.) from front of each side panel. Slide third pencil through holes.

Brake

8. *Anchor:* Punch a small hole in center of back panel. Feed small elastic from throwing arm through hole and secure with toothpick.

Anchor

9. *Cradle:* With an elastic band, fasten spoon to back of throwing arm, so cupped part faces front of catapult.

Cradle

Now, hold the frame steady, load the cradle with a marshmallow and slowly pull back the throwing arm. Ready, aim, fire!!

Jessica Scott Kerrin never did learn how to climb a rope. But she does have a huge collection of do-it-yourself books that she picked up at yard sales. Jessica learned about building catapults from one such book, and made a catapult that she  now uses to hurl tasty treats to the fish in her backyard pond in Halifax, Nova Scotia.

 Like Martin's mom, **Joseph Kelly** prefers old keyboards. He uses one to write songs for his wife. Though he enjoyed drawing all the swirled and speckled ice-cream flavors for Martin and his friends, when Polar Pete's ice-cream truck comes to Sonoma, California, Joseph will have a scoop of plain vanilla.

Catch up on all of Martin's adventures!

"Realistic, everyday situations, likable characters and simple stories written in rich language with solid dialogue and humor."
— **Kirkus Reviews**

HC ISBN:
978-1-55337-688-0

PB ISBN:
978-1-55337-772-6

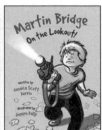

HC ISBN:
978-1-55337-689-7

PB ISBN:
978-1-55337-773-3

HC ISBN:
978-1-55337-961-4

PB ISBN:
978-1-55337-962-1

HC ISBN:
978-1-55337-976-8

PB ISBN:
978-1-55337-977-5

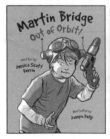

HC ISBN:
978-1-55453-148-6

PB ISBN:
978-1-55453-149-3

HC ISBN:
978-1-55453-156-1

PB ISBN:
978-1-55453-157-8

HC ISBN:
978-1-55453-158-5

PB ISBN:
978-1-55453-159-2

HC ISBN:
978-1-55453-160-8

PB ISBN:
978-1-55453-161-6

PB $6.95 US / $6.95 CDN • HC $16.95 US / $16.95 CDN

Written by Jessica Scott Kerrin • Illustrated by Joseph Kelly

WITHDRAWN
FROM THE COLLECTION OF
WINDSOR PUBLIC LIBRARY